Bike Thief

Bike Thief

Rita Feutl

orca soundings

ORCA BOOK PUBLISHERS

Library and Archives Canada Cataloguing in Publication

Feutl, Rita, 1959-, author
Bike thief / Rita Feutl.
(Orca soundings)

Issued in print and electronic formats.
ISBN 978-1-4598-0570-5 (bound).--ISBN 978-1-4598-0569-9 (pbk.).--
ISBN 978-1-4598-0571-2 (pdf).--ISBN 978-1-4598-0572-9 (epub)

I. Title. II. Series: Orca soundings
PS8611.E98B55 2014   jc813'.6   C2013-906724-8
                              C2013-906725-6

First published in the United States, 2014
Library of Congress Control Number: 2013952668

Summary: Injured in a car accident that killed their parents, Nick and his sister
are in foster care. Forced into stealing bikes to repay a debt,
Nick gets involved with a violent criminal gang.

MIX
Paper from
responsible sources
FSC® C016245
www.fsc.org

*Orca Book Publishers is dedicated to preserving the environment and has
printed this book on Forest Stewardship Council® certified paper.*

Orca Book Publishers gratefully acknowledges the support for its publishing
programs provided by the following agencies: the Government of Canada through
the Canada Book Fund and the Canada Council for the Arts,
and the Province of British Columbia through the BC Arts Council
and the Book Publishing Tax Credit.

Cover image by Getty Images

ORCA BOOK PUBLISHERS
PO Box 5626, Stn. B
Victoria, BC Canada
V8R 6S4

ORCA BOOK PUBLISHERS
PO Box 468
Custer, WA USA
98240-0468

www.orcabook.com
Printed and bound in Canada.

17 16 15 14 • 4 3 2 1

To Gordon, who happily joins me on all our cycling adventures, come rain, mud or sunshine.

Chapter One

"I'll pay you back. I promise."

"Yeah, right. Just waiting for that trust fund to kick in now that you turned sixteen? Gimme a break." Dwayne sneers. He turns and heads into the back of the pawnshop.

My arm aches. I set the shattered flat-screen TV gently on the counter. Right next to a perfect, unbroken, forty-two-inch model with a two-hundred-dollar price tag. They're identical. Except for the broken screen.

"Can't you use this one for parts?" I ask. Dwayne snorts.

I'm desperate. "This isn't for me, Dwayne, this is for Katie. She's freaking out. She thinks we'll get kicked out of this foster home."

Dwayne turns around. "How old is she these days?"

I don't like where this is going. "She's about to turn twelve," I say warily. "She's still in elementary school."

"Popular, your sister?"

"I dunno. I guess." Truth is, Katie is pretty cute, in that little sister sort of way. Even after all the stuff that's happened to us in the last year, she always has a smile for everyone. Even me. Especially me. And that's why I'm trying to replace this shattered TV with a new one before the Radlers come home. Katie didn't mean to knock the fireplace tongs into it. She was just showing me her new soccer move. But things went flying, and now Katie is going nuts. She really doesn't want to upset this set of foster parents. They're the only ones to agree to take both of us in. Together.

"Good," Dwayne says. "We can use her. Here's the deal."

I freeze. I'm creeped out. This smells of sex—or drugs. It's time for me to rock and roll right out of here. I don't know what Dwayne is offering. But if it involves Katie, I want no part. I pick up the TV. My shoulder throbs, but I ignore it.

"Hang on a minute, Nicky."

I cringe. Nobody calls me Nicky. I'm Nick. Nicholas to my teachers, but Nick to everyone else. I turn to the door.

"All I want is for you to get to know some of the kids she hangs out with.

I need some product. And some little runts to supply it."

What? Kids to *supply* the product? Usually, it's the other way around—kids to *buy* product. "Are we talking drugs here?" I'm curious in spite of myself.

Dwayne shrugs, and I watch the tattooed snakes ripple up his arms. "Nah, nothing like that. You're good with your hands, right?"

I set the TV back down again and nod. I can put anything together if you give me the time. I built my own fixie—fixed-gear bike—with some parts I bought from Dwayne's shop. That's how we know each other.

"Tell you what, Nicky. Just for you, I'll let you have the TV for a hundred bucks. And all you gotta do is find some kids who are willing to pick up some product for me. Product that their owners don't seem to want. Your job is to mix it up, and I'll sell it once you're done. TV's paid off in no time."

"What kind of product?"

"Bikes, Nicky. I want bikes. And the more expensive, the better."

Chapter Two

Katie's face lights up when I walk in the back door.

"You did it!" she says. She dances around me. "I'm so glad. I was really worried they'd come home while you were gone. I don't want to get into trouble, Nick. I really want us to stay together."

I put the flat-screen down on the stand and nod. The Radlers are strict.

And Katie already has two strikes against her. Last week she tried to heat a burger wrapped in foil. It made their microwave explode. Yesterday, she let the kettle boil dry. She isn't allowed to go into the kitchen by herself anymore. No wonder she's nervous.

"Look, I cleaned up all the broken glass. But there's a chunk of wood missing from the coffee table."

I check out the nick in the wood. This one's easy. "You still have your crayons?"

While she goes to find them, I attach the TV cables and press the remote. The screen shimmers on, good as new. I wait for Katie.

The crayon trick is my dad's. An image of him in our old garage flashes into my mind, and suddenly I'm almost drowning under a huge wave of…what? Homesickness? Sadness? I close my eyes and wait out the wave.

"Here." Katie thrusts something into my hands. I open my eyes. Her crayon case is jammed with junk. I dig through the tiny erasers, pencil crayons, grizzly-bear buttons, broken earrings and bits of paper. Why do girls carry all this stuff around? Finally, I find a brown wax crayon the same shade as the coffee table. I rub it against the raw wood until the surface looks smooth.

"Hey, that's great, Nick. I can't even tell." Katie eyes the table critically. She hugs me, but gently. She knows how much everything still hurts. "This is going to work. We'll make it work, won't we?"

I nod. "Let's get rid of the rest of the evidence," I say. I drop the crayon back into the pencil case. A slip of paper peeks out from one side. *Do u like me?* it says. I pull it out. At the bottom it says, *Yes, no, maybe?*

"So who's this for?" I wave the note at Katie.

"Hey, gimme that." She reaches for it, but I hold it high over her head.

"Not till you tell me," I say.

"It's mine!" Katie jumps for the note, then stumbles back. I grab her just before she goes flying into the TV. Again.

"Take it outside, you two. You shouldn't be horsing around in the living room." Katie and I freeze. How long has Mrs. Radler been standing in the doorway?

I look around the room. Just me, my sister and a pencil case. Nothing out of the ordinary. But a little distraction won't hurt. "I could bolt that flat-screen to the wall, Mrs. Radler. I'm good with my hands."

She looks at me in surprise. Normally, I don't say much around here. "Then use those hands to help me carry in the groceries. I swear I'm feeding an army."

I give Katie back the note. But not before I see the *Love, Alex* on the back. I grin. This is a note *to* my sister, not *from* her.

And then I realize I know him. Three times a week, I ride over to Katie's school to take her to her babysitting job. One kid is always there with her. Short kid. Showing off in front of her. Full of questions about my bike.

Bingo! I've found my first runt. This is going to be easier than I thought.

Chapter Three

The next day I skip social studies and ride my fixie to the meeting with Dwayne. I zip around to the back of an abandoned strip mall, tires humming. He's standing in the shadows, swinging a set of keys. I skid to a stop right next to him. Pebbles go flying.

"Smart-ass," he says. I can't tell if he's mad or not, so I don't say anything.

Dwayne unbolts the door and steps into what looks like a long, dark cave. He switches on a light. I follow, pushing my bike inside.

The place is big, gloomy and smells of mold. One bare bulb dangles from the ceiling, casting more shadows than light. We're in a boarded-up store. I can barely see a row of dingy counters at the front, but there's way more interesting stuff at the back…stuff that has my heart racing. The place is littered with bikes and bike parts. A tangle of handlebars lies next to a pile of wheel rims. Bike chains spill from an old box like a mess of snakes trying to escape. A titanium seat post leans against one wall. My mouth is watering. This is cycle heaven.

"Welcome to the Den, Nicky. Your job here is to put a few bikes together that I can either sell at the shop or Trevor can put online."

"Who's Trevor?" I kneel down to examine some bike pedals. Some of them are sitting in a puddle of water. Looking closer, I can see where a water stain runs down the concrete wall.

"He's the boss. He runs the place."

"Doesn't look like he really cares about it," I say, tracing my finger up the water stain.

The punch comes out of nowhere. My head slams into the wall. Before I can react, Dwayne yanks me up and swings me around and against the wall. "You disrespect Trevor, you disrespect me," he says. "Don't do it, if you know what's good for you. Do we understand each other?"

He's so close, I can smell his breath. It's rank. Dwayne's about my height, but he has at least fifteen years and thirty pounds on me. I'm not scrawny, but my rehab didn't involve beat downs. I nod.

"Good." His snakebite piercings glint as he steps back. "Now that we're on the same page about Trevor, let's see how we are on bike products."

The punch rattles me, but I take a deep breath. I can't back out now, I think. I look around. How hard can this be?

For the next hour, Dwayne quizzes me. I know bikes—cheap ones, pricey ones, road bikes, mountain bikes. I love them all—their feel, their speed, their control, their silence. A little rubber and metal is all you need to be flying down a trail in a hidden ravine or along a major roadway. It's the sweetest kind of freedom. Especially for me. On a bike, I can move. No limping. No half steps. It's as if things are almost back to normal.

"Don't waste your time on department-store crap," Dwayne says. "I need flash bikes I can sell at the shop, and Trevor wants expensive components to put online. You and your runts will pick up bikes around town and bring them back here. You'll pull them apart and rebuild them, so the serial number won't match up with the original bike. Leftover components go online."

I nod. I'm trying to ignore a voice in the back of my head. We didn't go to church much when Mom and Dad were…around. But we did talk about right and wrong, and *Thou shalt not steal* was right up there. We're talking about theft here. Taking something that isn't yours—

"Hey, Nick-eee." Dwayne drawls out the final syllable. I snap back to reality. "I'm serious about that hundred bucks. I'll need it by the end of next week."

"What?"

"Well, whaddya think? The guy that brought in the TV wants his money. Until you pay me, I can't pay him."

I swallow. I have eleven dollars in the toe of Dad's dress shoes. I didn't realize

I'd have to pay Dwayne so soon. The look he gives me is almost one of pity.

"Look, Nicky. Zone in here. I'm gonna do you a favor. I'm sending you Danny. Tomorrow night. He'll take you to the university. He's thirteen. One of my older runts."

"The university?"

"Best place for bikes. Those students claim to be poor, but their mommies and daddies give 'em great bikes. Which they're too drunk to lock up half the time. If you get me ten good bikes by the end of next week, we'll be square."

I nod. Okay. How hard can that be?

"But remember, these bikes better be good. And you're gonna need more than Danny. The more runts you find, the faster you'll fill the quota."

"Why do you call them runts?"

"Trevor calls 'em that. They're between eleven and thirteen, and they don't usually have criminal records, so they mostly float under the radar of the cops."

"So why does Trevor call them that?"

Dwayne seems to ignore me. He holds up a set of keys. "These are for the Den," he says. "You can work here whenever you want."

He tosses them to me and turns to walk out, then circles back. "I think he calls them runts because they're the weakest link in this business. Like those tiny pigs in a litter. And because they're so weak, they're easy to get rid of."

I swallow and nod slightly. But he's not done. "And by the way, you want to keep this whole bike-supply process here"—he glances around the Den—"under wraps. We don't want word getting out. Otherwise, people can get hurt."

He stares hard at me. "Now go find some runts of your own."

Chapter Four

Some kid is working on wheelies on Katie's mountain bike when I get to her school. I'm pretty sure it's Alex.

"Keep the handlebars straight when you come down," she shouts as he goes by.

That's my girl, I think proudly. I taught her that years ago. Back when—

"Hi, Nick." The kid props Katie's bike carefully against the curb, takes Katie's helmet off and comes over. "Your ride's just, just…" He searches for words.

"Awesome? Sweet? Sick? Cool?" Katie joins us. "Yeah, my brother knows how to build 'em. This is Alex, by the way."

I nod. Here's my chance to pull in my first runt. "I could show you how to build your own," I say carefully.

Katie looks at me and frowns. "How are you going to show him anything? You don't have the garage anymore."

"I've found another place," I say.

"How about today?" Alex is eager to start.

"Let me ride with Katie to her baby-sitting job," I say. "Where will you be in half an hour?"

"Right here. I won't go anywhere till you come back." He sits down on the curb in front of the school. Then he jumps up again. "But I don't have any parts. I've got nothing to…to start with."

"No problem, Alex," I say, grinning at him. "I think we can lay our hands on something."

Katie takes her helmet from Alex, snaps it on and climbs onto her bike. "Let's go, Nick. Mrs. Lamont gets all snotty if I'm late."

I nod at Alex. "I'll be back soon. And if you know anyone else who wants to learn about bikes, they can come too." I push off. We're halfway up the block before Katie says anything.

"Since when do you want to teach twelve-year-olds how to build bikes?" she asks. "You barely let me into the garage on Grange Street."

Just the mention of Grange Street hits me like a sucker punch. My feet nearly tangle with my pedals. I try to breathe, to think. "That wasn't just a place on Grange Street," I finally say. "That was our home."

"Exactly." Katie seems to pick up speed. I find my pedals and pump to keep up. "It *was* our home. But it's not anymore. Now it's with the Radlers. Where you don't have a garage to work in. What are you up to?"

How can Katie think of the Radlers' house as our home? I try to focus on riding, on not thinking about what happened to our home, to our family. But it's like pushing away the wind. "Don't you miss them?" I ask.

Katie slams on her brakes. I have to circle back to her. She's dropped her bike onto the curb and is standing beside it, her fists curled into balls. Her brown eyes are blazing, and her hair glows almost red in the September sunshine.

"Do I miss them? Are you kidding? I miss them every single day. I miss them in the morning when no one musses my hair at breakfast. And when I open my lunch bag and there's no cartoon in it. And in the evening..." She swallows hard. "Of course I miss them, you idiot. And it was even worse when you were stuck in that hospital, all banged up and completely out of it. But now you're here. And I'm not alone. And neither are you. Okay? And I don't want anything to wreck it."

I almost laugh. She doesn't want anything to *wreck* it? Everything *is* wrecked, since the day of the car *wreck* a year ago. My body is wrecked. Our family is wrecked. Our whole lives are wrecked.

So many bad things happened on that awful day. Trust me, I've had lots of time to add them up.

First thing? Arguing with my dad about mowing the stupid lawn that day. I'd forgotten—again—and he was furious. That's why he wasn't paying attention to the road.

Second thing? A drunk driver.

Third thing? The drunk driver roaring through a red light.

Fourth thing? Him slamming into the driver's side of our car.

Fifth thing? Mom was in the back, behind Dad, because I was riding shotgun.

Sixth thing? The drunk driver never put his foot on the brake, so our car was pushed into a lamppost on my side.

Seventh thing? My parents died before the ambulances got there.

Eighth thing? I couldn't do anything to help them because my right side was smashed up from my shoulder to my shinbone.

Ninth thing? The drunk driver walked away.

The only good thing about that day? Katie wasn't in the car. She was at the library, looking for picture books about bears. Katie has a thing about bears.

Well, bears and soccer. And on that day, Katie was working on a cartoon about bears that played soccer. So she spent that afternoon far away from all the wreckage.

"Nick! Are you there? Hello?"

I force myself to focus. I have to do this a lot since the accident. I shake my head.

"Fine, don't tell me," she snaps. "I've gotta go. Mrs. Lamont's going to kill me if I'm late." She climbs back onto her bike and pedals away. I trail behind. Once she wheels her bike into the Lamonts' backyard, I turn around. I have a runt to train.

Chapter Five

Alex is waiting just about where we left him, on the curb in front of the school. Another boy sits next to him. Two runts for the price of one? This is going to be easy. I pull up beside them.

"Who's this?" I ask.

"This is Stevie. He's in grade five," Alex says. He turns to the boy. "See, I told you he has a sweet ride." Stevie just nods.

Alex jumps up. "You're gonna show us how to build one just like it, right?"

"Pretty much," I say. "It depends on what we have to work with." I wonder how to get them to the Den. It's the best place to explain about getting product, I think.

"So where's this garage?" Alex asks. It's as if he can read my mind.

"You guys fast?" I ask. They nod. "Well, stick close."

I ride slowly so they can keep up. They're pretty good runners. In fifteen minutes, we're turning the corner of the abandoned building. A bulkier, bigger kid is kicking stones against the door of the Den.

"Who are you?" I ask.

The boy looks me over, then Alex and Stevie. "I'm Danny. Dwayne said for me to talk to you."

I pull the keys from my jacket pocket and unlock the door. This is turning into a real operation—that TV will be paid off in no time. I push my bike in and turn on the light.

"Cool!" Alex and Stevie inspect everything. They talk eagerly about the bikes they want to build. Danny slouches against the door, his hands in his pockets.

"So where do we start? Can I use this?" Alex drags over an aluminum frame. Danny snorts.

"What's so funny?" Alex drops the frame and goes up to the bigger kid. I have to hand it to Alex. He seems to have no fear.

Danny doesn't move from the door. "Aluminum's crap. If you're going to build yourself a bike, you want titanium. Or carbon fiber."

I sneer. "Yeah, as if you'll find titanium bikes lying around." Those ones are really high-end, for serious athletes or rich old guys who only go out on weekends and lock their rides up the rest of the time.

Alex swings around to me. "You got any of that here?"

I shake my head. Here goes, I think. "Nope, we've got to find ourselves some." I'm hoping they get the idea. About the bike parts. Or what Dwayne calls "the product."

"How?" Stevie speaks for the first time.

"It's all over the place," says Danny. "You just gotta grab some."

"Are we gonna *steal* bikes?" Alex frowns and looks at me. Suddenly, I feel...what? Dirty? Sleazy? Here's this kid with a crush on my sister, and I'm using him. And his friend. But I need the money. And it's not like I'm pushing drugs.

Danny snorts. "You mean none of you has ever lifted anything before?" He glares at us, as if we're guilty of some crime. "A chocolate bar from a checkout counter? Five bucks from your old lady's purse?"

Danny's beginning to bug me.

"I took a pack of gum once," says Alex. "But—"

"Crap. You mean I have to show you losers everything?" Danny takes a breath. "Look. Stealing bikes is easy. Half the time, the bikes aren't even locked up. It's like they're begging for someone to take them."

"But lots are locked up," says Stevie.

Danny snorts again. "Yeah, but the locks are mostly useless. All you need are these and it's game over." He pulls some bolt cutters from his pocket. The boys crowd around him.

"You also need to know what kind of bikes to look for," I say. I feel like I have to step in here. Danny's starting to run the show. The boys turn back. "Who knows what a Yeti is?"

Alex's eyes light up. "It's a big hairy monster who lives way up north with the polar bears," he says.

"Yup, but it's also a bike. A high-end bike. You guys need to look for expensive bikes, like Yetis or Giants or Rocky Mountains or Treks."

"And look for any components made of titanium or carbon fiber," Danny adds.

Stevie makes a face. "Titanium? Carbon fiber? How can I tell?"

"You gotta read it, dork," Danny says. "They make it easy for us. They write it right on the frame or the rim."

"Stevie's not so good at reading," Alex says.

I jump in. "Carbon fiber looks like there's a net wrapped around it."

"And if it's titanium, you just gotta think of girls," Danny says.

Stevie looks puzzled.

"The word starts *T-I-T*, you dork-head. Just think of tits."

The boys snicker. I'm getting tired of Danny. I shut them up with my next question.

"Who wants to try picking up some product with me tomorrow morning?" I turn to Danny. "Just so we're not complete losers when you show us the ropes."

Because really, how hard can it be?

Chapter Six

A girl with a ponytail jumps off her bike, takes the lock from her backpack and runs it through the school bike rack. I can tell she's late and she's rushing.

"That's the one," I say. My leg hurts a little. Alex and I walked to Wilfrid Laurier High School this morning. It's the Catholic high school in the neighborhood. I go to Diefenbaker High, the public school ten blocks away. I don't want our first stab at picking up "product" to take place on my home turf.

The girl forgets to snap the lock into place.

"I won't even need the cutters," Alex says.

The final bell rings, and the girl swings her backpack over her shoulder. The strap breaks just as she reaches the door. Her books tumble out. I'm beginning to feel sorry for her.

"Shit!" We can hear her from here. She stoops to pick up her stuff. The door swings open as two guys saunter out, and her books go flying again.

"This is like watching a TV show, but funnier," says Alex, snickering.

I cuff him on the back of the head. "Just keep your nose down and do what I told you," I say. "I'll meet you at the Den." I watch him tug off the girl's lock, climb on and pedal away. No one notices. I pull my hoodie up and start scoping out the other bikes. At the very least, I need a ride back.

"How's it going, Ni-i-ck-eeee?" It's Dwayne. I refuse to turn around. "I'm having a bit of trouble with this damn thing," Dwayne says. "The pedals keep turning, and there're no brakes." Dwayne rolls by me, and my guts start to churn. He's riding my fixie.

He grins. "Just checking up on you. You left this at the Den to bring that kid over here, so I thought I'd see what was so special about this bike. Maybe I could get part of the payoff by selling it. Most of this is steel, but the fork's carbon fiber. Thirty bucks might cover it. I mean, it's just a bunch of parts from old bikes. And you don't even have brakes. Maybe twenty dollars?"

I swallow. I built this bike by myself. But Dad was there for me the whole time, helping me with the design and working beside me in the garage, always ready to lend a hand. There isn't much else left from our time together. I was in rehab for five months after the accident. By the time I came out, almost everything was sold or gone. I have his dress shoes, his watch and this bike.

"Give it back, Dwayne."

"Nah. I'll let you limp along and think about your repayment schedule. I'll meet you at the Den. We'll see what you and your runt picked up." He lurches away on my bike, struggling with the pedals, looking like a dork who's never ridden a fixie.

I want to punch something. I want to run after him and pound him. I want to beat the crap out of him. He's an asshole, and he's riding my bike. I stumble along the street, not watching where I'm going. When I bash my sore leg into a bike leaning against a fence, I want to scream.

Instead, I look at the make. A Giant. Not bad. And it's unlocked. I pull it away from the fence and jump on.

My career as a bike thief has begun.

Chapter Seven

Alex and Dwayne are already in the Den when I ride up. I push the bike inside. Dwayne begins to clap. Slowly and loudly. The clapping echoes in the space.

"What are we celebrating?" Two men have come up behind me and are standing in the doorway.

"Hey, Trevor, we've got some product for you," says Dwayne. "I was applauding my friend here. He just brought in his first bike."

The men make their way into the Den. The big guy is bald, with a diamond stud in his ear. He has shoulders the size of a minivan. The other guy is smaller, with long, greasy hair. He has a scar on his cheek, and he keeps his sunglasses on even in the gloom of the Den.

"Three bikes. Nice." The big guy looks around.

I do the math. "No, the fixie's mine," I mutter. My voice sounds small to me, but the big guy hears.

"That true, Dwayne?"

Dwayne grins. "We've discussed selling it, Trevor, but we haven't settled on a price yet."

Trevor grunts. "Everything has a price." He walks around the Den, kicking at the bike parts. "My friend here is looking for a Yeti suspension platform. A late-model one. You got any of those?"

I shake my head. I already know exactly what's in the Den, and I haven't seen an expensive component like that. Trevor sighs. Then he walks over to the bike Alex just brought in. It's sitting against a counter.

"Well, this is a piece of crap. But I'll take the tires." He turns to me. "Five bucks. Pull 'em off."

I know the tires are good. I noticed them right away when that girl rode past. The tires are new. Worth about forty dollars each. And I thought I'd be getting ten bucks a bike. Ten bikes to make a hundred dollars.

"Do it," Dwayne mutters.

"Ten bucks," I say. "They're worth way more."

Trevor looks at me. "A runt with attitude," he says. He comes up close to me. I realize, suddenly, that I have no way out. From the corner of my eye, I see Alex slip out the door. I can't move.

The other guy in the shades? He doesn't say anything. He just watches.

"Fine. Seven fifty," Trevor says finally. He digs into his pocket and throws the money on the counter. A quarter rolls onto the floor and into the darkness. "But I want you to get me that Yeti platform. Soon. Now strip those tires off."

I find a tire lever and go to work. It bothers me that I'm pulling these tires off for so little money. It bothers me that I owe so much money. But what bothers me the most? The fact that Trevor just called me a runt.

Chapter Eight

I'd planned to give Dwayne the seven fifty, but hc leaves with Trevor. Instead, the money stays in my pocket and I rebuild the Giant. I trade out parts so that when I'm done, it's a different bike. Even if the owner reports the serial number, it'll look so different that he'll never recognize it. I set it by the back door for Dwayne to pick up.

The other bike—the one I stripped the tires from—looks all pitiful and pathetic. What's left of it is probably useless. But I stuff it behind some other bike frames, lock the door and leave. It's late afternoon, and I'm starving. Katie goes to a friend's house on Tuesdays, so I'm on my own.

The smell of something delicious floats past as I ride along the avenue. My stomach growls. Ida's Diner is up ahead, and Ida makes the best chili I've ever tasted. Except for my mother's. Mom used to say her secret ingredient was chocolate, but that's crazy. Who puts chocolate in their chili?

I give my head a shake. I have to stop with the memories. I focus on Ida's chili. It's just what I need. I lock my bike in front of the diner, pop the seat off and carry it inside with my helmet.

Ida's Diner is great. It has red-checked plastic on the tables and this cool mask on the wall over the door. Today, the front seems really crowded and busy, with people milling around. One person's even under a table, wiping up what looks like spilled chili. I pick a spot at the back of the diner.

"You just missed the show," an old guy at the table next to me says. "The new girl dropped a plate all over a customer's lap. He kept shouting. She kept apologizing. Ida had to come out from the back and settle everybody down."

"Stop being such a gossip, Earl," says Ida, coming over. "That's my niece Mandy you're talking about." She sets a basket of warm bread in front of me. "You in for my chili, Nick?"

I nod. I don't come in often, but Ida knows how much I like her chili. A minute later, a bowl of heaven slids in front of me. Earl applauds. I look around, surprised.

"Hey, you didn't get a lapful," Earl says, nodding at my meal and then at my server, who hasn't moved.

I look up. Standing in front of me, looking like she's trying not to cry, is the girl from this morning. The one with the ponytail. The one whose bike I have in the Den a block and a half away. Minus two tires.

"Please, just let me stand here for a minute," the girl says quietly. "I've just had such a shitty day, and I need a minute. Can we pretend we know each other?"

A huge tear rolls off her chin and plops onto the table. "So, sit," I say before I know what I'm doing.

She wipes her face and looks at me. You could swim in those eyes, I think. And not because of the tears. Her eyes are the same golden brown as the freckles across her nose. The freckles are cute. She's cute. "I'm Nick," I say. What am I doing?

She smiles. "I'm Mandy," she says. "Have we met somewhere before?"

Oh, shit. Did she see me this morning? "Don't think so," I say. I grab a spoon and start to shovel in chili. But it's so hot, I have to spit it back into my bowl. Mandy hurries away and comes back with a glass of ice cubes.

"Take one of these and hold it where it hurts," she says.

"You don't have an ice cube big enough," I say. Where did that come from?

Mandy looks at me, puzzled.

"Miss? Can we get our bill?"

She's gone. I eat the chili. It's good, now that it's cooler. Mandy comes back with a water jug. She sloshes some into my glass, and an ice cube skitters across the table. It lands in my lap. She lunges for it at the same time I do. We bump heads. At the next table, Earl is laughing so hard he's wheezing. Mandy scuttles into the kitchen. I swipe the ice cube onto the floor.

"Hey, Ida! Your niece has a thing for dumping stuff into customers' laps," Earl calls out.

Mandy's wail drifts out through the swinging kitchen door. Earl tries to catch my eye. Instead, I wipe up the last bit of chili with a piece of bread. Delicious.

The kitchen door swings open. Mandy comes out, slaps my bill on the table and turns. She steps on the melting ice cube. As she crashes toward Earl's table, the grin on his face fades to fear. I rise, grab one of Mandy's flailing arms and pull her back toward me. The restaurant cheers.

I just have time to feel the beating of her heart through the soft skin of her wrist before Ida steps between us. "There's a kid outside who says he knows you. But I'd stay away from him. He's trouble."

I look out the diner window. Danny's standing there, waving at me to come out.

Chapter Nine

"Classes start in an hour," says Danny. "We gotta round up the others and get down there."

I'm confused. School's out. Why's this kid talking about classes?

"The bikes. We need to get more bikes," he says, as if I'm slow on the uptake. "The best time to get them at the university is after classes start. It's still light enough to look for the right stuff but dark enough that we can hide."

I turn away to undo my locks. Danny's being bossy, and it's really beginning to grate on me, but I don't say anything until I've slid my seat back on. "I'm taking my bike to the Den. Round up the other two and meet me at the subway station."

I wonder whether Alex will come out. He looked really scared when he left the Den this morning.

But all three boys are there when I show up at the subway station twenty minutes later. We slide through the turnstiles and catch a train right away. The younger boys are quiet.

"We all good?" I ask.

"What if I get caught?" Stevie asks.

Danny rolls his eyes. "You're not even twelve yet. Nothing's going to happen. Haven't you ever been in trouble before?"

"Not with the police," Stevie says.

"No sweat then," Danny says. The two younger boys look at me. I nod. But I'm not so sure.

We get off at the university station. Even in the gathering darkness, we can see that the campus is littered with bikes. "It's like a freaking candy store," Danny says. "Just remember, expensive bikes. Delta7s, Yetis—"

"And *T-I-T* tits," Stevie pipes up.

I cuff him. "Grow up, will you?"

I turn to Danny. "We'd better split up. Make sure you get him back to the Den, okay?"

Danny nods. He and Stevie turn left and head toward the side of a huge building where dozens of bikes nuzzle against each other like ponies in a corral.

Alex walks ahead, letting his fingers slide along whatever he passes—a wall, a railing, a bike. He stops to look at the bike. "Magna?"

"Keep going."

We pass a mostly black road bike clamped to a fence. But the clamp only attaches to the frame. The removable front wheel is free. So is the leather seat. "We'll stop by on the way back," I say.

We keep walking. Students rush past, lugging books and backpacks. Looking like they're late for class. My parents always said I'd go here one day. And look—I've made it! Here I am…learning…how to be a criminal!

Alex spots the Giant first. A flimsy cable lock snakes through the frame and front wheel and onto a bike rack. He whips out the bolt cutters but struggles to slice through the cable. I take them from him and clamp them closed. My shoulder twinges, but I ignore it.

"Get on it, Alex, and head back."

"I don't know the way," Alex says.

I don't want him hanging around here with a stolen bike. "Wait for me at that Dumpster over there, okay?"

Alex nods. I turn away. Suddenly, I want to be far away from here, away from this scene of the crime, away from where someone can put a hand on my shoulder and accuse me of stealing. But I have to get another bike. Another eight bikes, just to pay off my debt to Dwayne.

I find the next one a block away. I can't believe my eyes. It's a Yeti, with the suspension platform that Trevor's buddy needs. Its frame is chained to a parking meter. Just the frame. I almost start to laugh. I wait while a guy walks by, then a man and a woman who are more interested in each other than anything on the street. When no one else comes down the sidewalk, I lift the bike and the chain right over the parking meter. People really are stupid, I think. I wrap the chain around the seat, climb on and head back to the Dumpster.

I don't see the red-and-blue flashing lights until I turn the corner.

Chapter Ten

I brake and melt into the shadows past the streetlight. Did they get Alex? Should I turn around?

I stop. I can't just leave Katie's friend hanging out to dry, can I? I move closer.

The broad back of a big campus cop blocks my view. He's looking down at something—or someone.

"Pssst! Nick!"

I jump. In the shadows next to me, something moves. I look closer. It's Alex. He's okay! I'm *so* relieved. Then Alex whispers, "It's Stevie. They stopped him because he didn't have a helmet."

I want to smack myself. Of course they would. Why didn't I think of that? Anyone under eighteen has to wear a helmet in this city. I don't have mine tonight, but I can get by. A kid like Stevie—he would stick out.

I watch glumly as a second campus cop holds open the door of the cruiser. Stevie climbs into the backseat. When the cop shuts the door, I can barely see the top of Stevie's head through the window.

This kid is younger than Katie. I can't let him get hauled away. I start to step out of the shadows, but something yanks me back.

"They're just gonna take him home," a voice mutters. Danny is right beside me, perched on a Cell Swift road bike. I watch as the cops stash a battered mountain bike in the trunk of the cruiser and then drive off.

"So, what did you find?" Danny asks, nodding at my ride.

I put Stevie out of my mind. "A Yeti," I say, all casual.

"And I went back for that front wheel and that seat," says Alex, bringing everything out from behind the Dumpster.

"Not bad," says Danny with grudging respect in his voice. I'm not sure I like it.

He pulls a helmet from his backpack and puts it on.

"Why didn't you tell the other two to bring a helmet?" I ask. "Stevie might not have been caught."

Danny smirks. "Can't think of everything," he says. "Besides, they're *your* runts, not mine." He pushes off into the darkness.

"What's a runt?" Alex asks.

I ignore him and set off. After tonight's haul, I just need five more bikes. Then I'll be done.

Chapter Eleven

My pillow feels hot and lumpy. The night is crawling by. Will Stevie give us up? Will the cops show up and drag me from the house—in front of the Radlers? In front of Katie?

As soon as it's light out, I dress, snap on my helmet and head off on my bike. I need to ride.

It's easy to dodge the early-morning joggers out trying to work off the pounds they put on sitting in their offices all day. I make my way to the bike path deep in the ravine, crunching over the falling leaves, breathing in the autumn air. I ride and ride, wheels thrumming on the pavement, making distance, flying, trying to escape. After an hour, I'm starving. The way home takes me right past Ida's Diner.

I don't have any money, but I pull up to the side of the building anyway. I watch through the window as Mandy grabs the coffeepot and heads for the tables at the back of the restaurant. Her ponytail bounces as she walks. I like that. I like the way—

"Hey, Nicky. What are you looking at?" Dwayne comes up next to me, puts his arm around my shoulder and drags me right to the middle of the window. I cringe. I don't want anyone to see me.

Mandy turns, looks at the two of us outside and waves at me.

"Aha!" Dwayne says gleefully. "I do believe our Nicky's got himself a girl-friend. Pretty little thing. I hear she lost a bike recently. Ida says she just spent good money on some new tires for her."

I shut my eyes. I'm not sure where this is going, but I know I don't want to be on the ride.

"Nick? There's a plate of bacon and eggs in here with your name on it." I open my eyes. Ida's at the door, looking at me. I swallow.

Dwayne moves his arm from my shoulder and slaps me on the back. "Sorry, Ida. He'll have to take a rain check. We've got a little business to settle first."

Ida looks directly at me. "You sure, Nick?"

I nod and turn away, from Dwayne, from the diner, from Mandy.

"Let's roll," I say. I climb onto my fixie and head to the Den, not bothering to wait for Dwayne.

Danny's talking to Trevor when I guide my bike through the door. "I keep telling you I won't push that stuff," he says slowly, "but just take a look at this bike. The rear derailleur alone is worth two hundred dollars new."

"But it's not new, is it?" Trevor says coolly. "I'll give you fifty bucks for the bike, and that's it."

I'm confused. They're talking about the bike Danny stole last night. With us. I figured it was one of the bikes I could use to pay off Dwayne. Obviously, Danny has other ideas.

"I don't have to sell it to you," Danny says. He sounds mad. "I could just sell it online myself and pay off what I owe you."

Dwayne steps past me. I didn't hear him come in, but suddenly he's there, grabbing Danny, shoving him to a wall and banging his head against it.

"What comes into the Den is ours," Dwayne says. "You got that?" He smacks Danny across the face. Hard. Blood trickles from Danny's nose.

Danny looks dazed. Trevor looks bored. I'm stunned. That's when Trevor's buddy walks in. The guy with the shades. The guy looking for the Yeti component.

"You found one," Shades says. He ignores the punch-up at the wall and heads straight to where I parked the bike yesterday. He's still wearing his sunglasses. The scar on his cheek twitches as he walks past me. He must be really excited about getting the part.

Dwayne gives Danny a final shake and lets him go. He and Trevor move to the Yeti. Danny wipes his face, then glares at me. I look away. My feet finally unglue from the floor. I set down my bike and move to the three men.

"Wrong bike, Nicky." Dwayne's grinning.

I look at the others. Shades finally speaks. "This is an SB66. Mine's an SB95. Way bigger wheels."

I nod. Of course. Trevor did mention a late model. But a bike's a bike. It still means money in my pocket. Or, at least, in Dwayne's pocket. The question is, how much.

"Take it apart," Trevor says. I want to ask how much I'm getting. But Dwayne is standing right behind me. He puts a hand on my sore shoulder and squeezes.

"You should see our Nicky strip down a bike," he says.

I slide away from his hand. "It's Nick," I say quietly.

Dwayne punches me playfully in the same shoulder. I keep my face frozen and pick up a wrench and a socket set.

"How long you been doing this, Nick?" Shades asks.

Dwayne jumps in. "He started with us just this week. But he knows his stuff, man."

I go to work. I lay out the bars, the stem, the fork and all the rest of it while they watch. A ride worth thousands of dollars, reduced to bare components.

Trevor pulls a fifty-dollar bill from a wad in his pocket and lets it flutter down next to the pedals. I stare at it. Dwayne swoops down. Scoops it up.

"This and the two bikes you brought in last night makes seventy dollars, Nicky. You're over the hump. Just another fifty to go."

I look at him. "I thought I only owed you a hundred."

Dwayne looks at Trevor. Nods at me. "Bright boy, our Nicky. You can tell he goes to school. He can add." He turns to me. "But you forgot about interest,

Nicky boy. The longer you take, the more you have to pay me back. Get us five more bikes and you're done. But get them fast."

Chapter Twelve

I skip classes and spend the day hunting
bikes on the other side of town. Cruising
from school to school. Checking out
bike racks at grocery stores. Noticing
bikes locked to lampposts, bus stops,
fence rails. If I see a likely prospect,
I lock up my own bike a block away,
then walk back to the new set of wheels
like I own it. Like it's mine. I only use

my bolt cutters once. The other two are unlocked, just begging to be taken. I ride off on them, pick up my own bike and head back to the Den. Then it's time to pick up Katie.

Alex is waiting at the curb with my sister. No Stevie. I haven't thought about Stevie since this morning.

"Guess what?" Katie jumps up as I skid to a stop. "Stevie got caught stealing a car!"

"It wasn't a car," says Alex.

Katie looks at him. "How do you know? Were you there?" Alex says nothing. Katie turns back to me. "And he had a gun. That's what Laura said. Stevie's mother came to the school this morning. Laura was in the office getting a late slip and she heard everything. He made the people get out of the car and then he jacked it." I can tell she's proud of being able to use the word *jacked*.

Alex rolls his eyes.

"Where's Stevie now?" I ask.

"They're sending him to a new school. Laura said his mother was crying."

"Get on your bike," I tell her. "Mrs. Lamont's waiting."

Alex looks at me. "Meet you at the Den?"

I nod and ride off. Katie chatters on beside me. My mind is a million miles away, wondering about what I'm doing. Funny how one little action seems to cause a whole bunch of other actions. One stupid broken TV leads to stolen bikes and a crying mother and—

"Nick? Nick! Who's this guy?"

I snap out of my thoughts. We always ride along the side streets, where the traffic is lighter. Cars usually skirt around us, leaving us some room. But a black Grand Cherokee is keeping pace, right beside us. I look over. Trevor's pal Shades stares back. He's alone. He looks from me to my sister and then does the oddest thing. He salutes me, steps on the gas and drives off.

"Nick! Who. Is. He." She says each word carefully, as if I have trouble understanding.

"Just some guy, okay? Can you hurry up? I've got places to go."

Katie is quiet for a moment. Then she says, "I know you're meeting Alex. Where do you guys go, anyway? Where is this Den? Maybe I should come too."

"No!" I shout. It's bad enough that Shades has seen Katie with me here in the street. The last thing I want is for her to get her mixed up with Dwayne and Trevor. I remember Danny's face this morning.

"I don't want you anywhere near there," I say. I have trouble getting my voice down to a normal level.

"Okay, okay. Calm down. Mrs. Lamont's gonna think we're fighting."

We pull into the Lamont driveway. Katie jumps off her bike. "Will you be home when I get in? You've been out a lot this week."

Home? Where's that? "I'll see, Katie." If I find two more bikes, I'm home free.

I wheel around and take off. I don't look back. Once again I'm flying, skimming along the surface of the earth, pedals spinning. Full tilt.

Which is, of course, when I see a girl with a ponytail step right into the street in front of me.

Chapter Thirteen

The thing about my fixie is that the drive chain and the cranks are directly connected. There's no spinning free-wheel, which means you can't ever coast. You're always pedaling. And the only way to brake is to lock your legs against the turning pedals and bring the back wheel to a skidding stop.

Five months ago, I could barely do this. My leg was so shattered, I could hardly get on the bike. But I'm stronger now. I pull up beside Mandy and skid. And then, just because I can, I spin around so I'm facing backward and keep pedaling—backward.

"Hey," I say.

"Hey yourself," Mandy says. She's moving pretty fast. I barely get a glimpse of her freckles before she strides across the street.

"What's the matter? Someone slip an ice cube down your shirt?" The words are out before I get a chance to think about them.

The start of a grin flickers across her face, but Mandy keeps walking. "I'm late. These days I'm always late. Someone stole my bike from school. So now I have to really book it to get to work on time."

I nearly stop pedaling. This is my fault. "So climb on," I say. "I'll give you a lift."

She looks at me but keeps walking. "My aunt says you hang out with people who are trouble."

I nod. Then I say, "I can't help it if you throw ice all over the place. Talk about trouble. You could have killed that old guy sitting at the next table."

She hits me. Lucky thing she's on my good side. But she's smiling. "You're...nice," she says finally—and keeps walking. I'm stunned. What do I say to that? A pedal smacks the back of my leg. I catch up to her. She can really move.

Ask a safe question, I tell myself. "How come you're always at the diner?"

"I live with my aunt. Just for now. My mother...she needs some time to herself," Mandy says. She looks directly at me, and the gold glints in her eyes

72

glow in the September sunshine. "Aunt Ida said I could live with her. But I can't just mooch off her. So I work before school and after school. Especially now. I need to buy another bike."

I have to do something. I pull ahead of her, lean forward on my handlebars, then crank backward on the pedals. I skid, jump off and bow down in front of her. "My chariot awaits you," I say.

"Is that thing even safe?"

I cross my heart. Then I hold out my hand so Mandy can use it to steady herself. She shifts her backpack to the front, climbs on and settles herself on my handlebars.

I push off, careful to hold my bike steady.

Mom used to grow these vines with small, colorful flowers by the back door. She called them sweet peas. In the summer, they were the first thing I smelled when I went out and the last thing I smelled when I went in. Mandy's ponytail smells of sweet peas. Good thing she's facing forward. She can't see the grin on my face.

We pull up to Ida's Diner. I can see Mandy's aunt through the window. She stops pouring coffee to look us over. I wave at her. Ida nods at me. It's a small nod. Then she turns away. Mandy climbs off the bike.

"Your hair," I say. "It smells…"

Mandy freezes. A frown creeps across her face.

"It smells like these little flowers my mom used to grow," I say. "Like sweet peas."

The frown disappears. "Why, thank you, kind sir," she says. As she goes inside, she's grinning too.

Chapter Fourteen

I head back to the Den, pumped. I have an idea. I want to rebuild Mandy's bike. Find her better tires than the ones Trevor took. Maybe a new set of cables. I'll leave it outside the diner. Maybe with a note that says *From a secret admirer*. Or maybe I'll just tell her *I* took it so I could build her a better bike.

I work out the details as I pull into the back of the building. Alex is at the door.

"Finally," he says. He kicks the door.

"What's your problem?" All my ideas about Mandy's bike shrivel up. Alex scowls at me.

"You were going to show me how to build a bike. A bike like yours. And so far, all I've done is learn how to steal bikes. And watch one of my friends get in trouble. And see his mother cry in the principal's office."

"Did Stevie mention you? Or Katie?" I unlock the door.

"Katie! What does Katie have to do with it? Is she in on this?" He follows me inside.

"No! Of course not. She doesn't know anything. I just don't want her to get in trouble."

Alex snorts. He sounds like Danny. "Sure. You don't want *her* to get into trouble. But me or Stevie...that's okay, right? Because we're just runts, right? The bottom of the pecking order." He kicks the nearest bike frame. It's Mandy's. I yank him away. I want to shake him, but an image of Dwayne flashes across my mind, and I let Alex go.

"Oh sure, pick on someone smaller than you—that's easy," says Alex. I can tell he's close to tears. "But you can't stand up to those other guys." His voice goes up a bit, and he adds a whine. "Don't pay me five dollars, Mr. Boss Man, sir. At least give me ten. They're worth way more than that."

"Shut up, Alex. You don't know anything about it," I say. A slow burn of anger creeps up from my gut. Who is this…this *runt* to make fun of me like this? All I want is to pay off the damn television set. But the problems keep spreading, like the broken lines on the screen after Katie made that kick. If I could just—

"Hey, Nick? Or should I call you Nick-eee?" Now Alex sounds like Dwayne, and it brings me back to the present.

"Don't," I say.

"Yeah, yeah. Otherwise, you'll beat me up. Well, forget it. I'm done. I'm done with you and I'm done with Katie. And I'm done with bikes." Alex pulls open the door, but before he goes through, he stops. "I don't get it. Katie thinks you walk on water. She adores you. But you're just a shitty brother and a really shitty guy."

After Alex leaves, I can't go near Mandy's bike. I try to rebuild at least one of the rides I picked up this morning, but my heart's not in it. The thrill's not there when I send a wheel spinning in its fork or when the smell of chain grease drifts my way. Mandy's bike leans against my work counter, crippled, stripped and useless. The cheap screwdriver I'm using bends as I try to pry away a component. I give up.

I climb on my fixie and head to the Radlers' house. I shoot along side streets, pedaling hard to empty out my head. I want the thrum of the tires to wipe out my worries. But when I turn onto the last street, I have to snap back to reality.

Katie's sitting outside on the Radlers' front steps. And my social worker's car is parked in the driveway.

Chapter Fifteen

"Where have you been?" Katie hisses. "They're looking for you."

A tingle of fear flows into my hands. They must know about the bikes. I'm busted. I want to kick myself. I thought I'd been pretty careful. I'd even put up my hoodie under my helmet so people couldn't see my face.

"There you are, Nick. We've been wondering where you were." Mr. Radler is standing at the door. Behind him, several more figures are waiting.

I think about jumping on my bike and riding away, but Katie takes it from me. "I'll lock up," she says.

Mr. Radler holds the screen door open for me. As I walk in, Mrs. Radler brings a tray into the living room. It's piled with buns. "We had pulled pork for dinner. These are still warm. There's an extra one here for you, Kris."

Kris is my social worker. I haven't seen him since the week after Katie and I moved in here. He's tall and skinny, and he does that thing where he hangs on to your hand for an extra half second when he shakes it. Then he stares at you, forever, like he's trying to see inside you. It's beginning to piss me off. I pull my hand away. "I'll just go wash up," I say. No one else says anything.

When I get back, everyone's in the living room. Even Katie. She's curled in a ball at the end of the couch, far from anyone else. I sit down beside her and grab a bun. If I'm going to be shot, I may as well eat my last meal. My hands shake as I try to put a napkin around the bun.

"I asked Kris to come over because I got a call about you today, Nick," says Mrs. Radler.

Well, here it comes, I think. I wonder whether I'll get a say about which one of those juvie group homes I'll have to go to. Will Katie be able to come visit? I cram half the bun into my mouth so I don't have to say anything.

"Your school has reported you absent for the last three days, Nick. What's going on?"

School? This is about school? I stop chewing and look up. Everyone's staring at me. Even Katie.

"Is something going on that we need to know about, Nick?" asks Mr. Radler. "Are you being bullied?"

I nearly snort the pulled pork out my nose. Bullying? They think I'm hiding from a few goons my age at school? If they only knew. I shake my head and swallow, then reach for another bun.

"Then what is it, Nick? Why aren't you at school?" Katie grabs my sleeve so I'll look at her.

"It's...it's nothing. I just felt like being outside. I wanted to ride. The weather's been so great, and my leg..." My voice drifts off. I'm hoping for some sympathy.

"Is your leg that sore, Nick? Are you doing your exercises? Do you need another appointment with the physio?" Mrs. Radler looks worried.

Katie smacks my arm. "You don't skip school for half a week and make up your own rehab," she says. "You're supposed to be good at school. Mom always said…"

I stand up and cut her off. "Don't you start telling me what Mom said." I'm angry again, and my voice goes up. "I remember exactly what she said."

"Then stop cutting classes," says Katie. "And stop feeling sorry for yourself."

"I am NOT feeling sorry for myself," I shout at her. Kris gets up from the other side of the room. Before he can grab me, I dash for the door.

"If I'm in any trouble, Katie, it's because of you. It's all your fault," I shout back. I see her face go white. Then I head out to my bike.

Chapter Sixteen

It's dark now, and I ride on the edges of weak pools of street light. Shadows chase me. Voices haunt me. I pedal and pedal, harder and harder. But I can't get away from any of it.

The dim outline of the Den's strip mall is up ahead. I let the pedals move my feet now instead of the other way around. I slow and turn the corner.

Trevor's white van, the one he uses to move bikes around, is parked next to the Den. A weak sliver of light seeps from the Den's open door. Low, angry voices rumble out from inside.

"They're not even in junior high yet. How can you lose them?" I recognize Dwayne's voice and decide I don't need to go inside just yet.

"*I* didn't lose them. They weren't *my* runts to lose. Ask your wonder boy, Nick the Dick. If he can strip a bike in ten minutes, he should be able to keep track of his own runts."

A new voice cuts in. Bigger. Deeper. It's Trevor. "I asked you to break them in, Danny. It was a personal favor to me."

Danny's voice is low when he speaks. "You weren't asking for a favor, Trevor. That was an order, like all the other orders you've made since I got sucked into your system. And now you want me to suck other runts in. I know how you operate. But they're not my runts. I will pay off my debts, but I'm not bringing in fresh meat."

"Watch your mouth, boy." Dwayne's voice climbs with each word. "You need to do exactly what Trevor tells you."

But Danny ignores him. "I know what you're up to. I see you guys doing the same thing to Dickhead. And it's the same thing you did to Joe. Now he's up to his eyeballs pushing cocaine. You're just getting us ready to run in your gang."

I'm stunned. Was that why Danny was being such a pain? He didn't want us getting involved? How could I have been so stupid? An operation like this couldn't just be about bikes. First stop, bike cranks…second stop, bags of crack?

Danny's voice drops so low, he's almost speaking to himself. "Problem is, I can't see a way out. Every time

I turn around, there's another thing owing—another 'favor' I need to do."

Dwayne laughs. "You think?"

"All the time," Danny shoots back. "You should try it. Just once, maybe."

In the shadows outside, I smile. I give Danny credit for balls. But inside, Trevor orders Dwayne to give Danny something else. "Teach him a lesson," he says.

Footsteps head toward the door. I panic. The last thing I want is to meet Trevor outside in the darkness. I'm halfway down the back alley when I hear the door slam shut. I look back. There's no one outside. Which means that both men are inside with Danny.

They'll kill him. I circle back on my bike. A whack thuds through the door. I feel sick. I wish I still had my cell phone. I wish I still had the old, broken TV. I wish I still had my old, unbroken life. I eye the end of the alley. It would be so easy to just leave…but I can't. I'm stuck here. I can hear punches on the other side of the door, and moans. Something bubbles up inside me.

I find a rock. I'm about to bang on the door with it when Trevor's voice cuts through the metal door.

"Enough. I have that meeting."

The sound of smacking stops. In the silence, I place the rock back on the pavement. Then I hear Dwayne's voice. "What'll we do with him?"

"We can't leave him here. Pack him in the back of the van."

I slip behind a Dumpster just before the door bangs open. Trevor unlocks the back doors of the van. Dwayne drags out Danny's limp body and shoves him in.

"I'll drive," says Trevor. "You get in the back with him."

Dwayne climbs in, and Trevor swings the doors shut. He gets in on the driver's side, and the headlights come on. As the van starts to move down the alley, I realize I have no choice. Letting Stevie deal with trouble by himself was bad enough. There's no way I'm abandoning Danny. I pedal as hard as I can, chasing after that van.

Chapter Seventeen

Bicycle messengers, or cycle couriers, made fixies popular. They looked at velodrome cyclists, who race in outdoor arenas at kick-ass speeds, and started using the same ride. A fixed-gear bike is stripped down to the bare essentials, so it has no shifters, cables, freewheel hubs or even brakes. That means it weighs a whole lot less than a normal bike. And that means a fixie goes way faster.

Which is a good thing, because that's just what I do. I keep Trevor's van in my sights as it cruises along the side streets and then pulls onto a main road. Traffic is pretty light, and I don't want them to see me, but I don't want to lose them either.

It's a tricky thing, riding a bike with no brakes. You have to be really aware of what's happening all around you, on the road, on the sidewalk, in the cars parked next to you. You have to time the lights and check the crossroad traffic. You don't want to waste all the speed you've just created because there's a red light up ahead. If you do, you're like some stupid driver who floors the gas pedal and then has to slam on the brakes. All that gas and speed—pointless.

But the lights are green, and I'm flying so fast that tears flow. I need to keep up. I need to see what they're doing with Danny. I need to make sure he'll be okay.

The van slows, signals and turns. As I come up to the turnoff, I realize I know this road. It leads down to a park by the river. I've been along this road, and the bike paths that feed into it, hundreds of times. I stop cranking on my pedals. I shoot by the turnoff, then circle back. The van's brake lights drop down into the valley. Then they stop moving.

Is this the meeting place Trevor talked about? Or are they getting rid of Danny here? I fight my pedals to ride slowly down the hill, careful not to make any noise. Halfway down, I see a Grand Cherokee illuminated in Trevor's headlights. I freeze. It's the same Grand Cherokee that Shades drives. The same one that drove beside me and Katie that day. I get off my bike and watch the figures below.

Shades steps forward into the head-lights. He's carrying a briefcase. Trevor kills the headlights and gets out of the van. It's dark now, but my eyes adjust. Shades lays the briefcase on the van's hood and snaps it open. It sounds like the *pop-pop* of TV gunfire. Trevor sets a matching case beside it and opens it.

I'm straining to see. What are they doing? Where's Danny in all of this? What's Dwayne doing? Should I ride a little closer?

My foot is fishing for my pedal when lights burst on behind Shades and a voice bellows, "Police! Show us your hands." One cop grabs Shades and two more step in front of him.

But before they can get to Trevor, the back of the van bursts open, and Dwayne steps out. He has one arm around Danny's neck. His other hand has a gun, aimed at Danny's head. Danny's face is covered in blood. He looks stunned.

"Get back! Get back, or I swear I'll shoot him," Dwayne screams.

For a moment, it's so quiet, I swear I can hear my heart beat. Then one of the cops yells, "Drop your weapon!"

But nobody moves. Trevor starts to laugh. "Thanks, guys. Not only do I get all my cocaine back, but I get the money too." He closes both briefcases and puts them into the van. "Put the runt back in," he says to Dwayne, who is still holding the gun to Danny's head.

From up the hill, I watch as Danny struggles not to be dragged back into the van. They're going to get away, I think. Dwayne and Trevor are going to walk away, just like the drunk guy who nailed my family.

Before I have time to think, I jump on my bike and barrel down that hill, aiming straight for Dwayne.

Chapter Eighteen

Danny may have a thing for carbon fiber or titanium bikes, but I built my fixie with a lot of steel. So when I slam into Dwayne, I have speed and heft on my side. I'm up on my pedals, leaning forward, and when the front tire catches the back of Dwayne's knees, his head snaps back. It's my helmet that takes most of the impact.

Arms and legs fly through the air. "Run, Danny, run," I scream. Danny picks himself up off the road and does exactly what I tell him. I'm still upright, and I pedal after him, past cops and headlights and the glint of guns and badges. We're off the bike path, plunging down toward the river. Danny just keeps going, and so do I.

When we're deep into the valley, far from the lights and the noise, Danny stops and rolls onto the grass next to the water.

"I can't do this anymore," he gasps.

I swing back uphill to stop. "You don't have to," I say. "I just wanted you to escape from Dwayne. We can go back now. Let the police handle it."

Danny groans and touches a gash in his lip. "Do you even know what the meeting was about?"

"Yeah. Drugs. I heard him. Cocaine."

"Well, at least you're not a total dickhead," Danny says. He gets up onto his knees and winces. "I think Dwayne broke my ribs back at the Den."

"Then let's go and talk to the cops," I say. Shouts and sirens drift by above us.

"I take it back. You really are a dickhead," Danny says, "Don't you understand? I'm involved. Hell, so are you. You think it's just bikes? Trevor runs a whole slick operation where he hooks in runts like you and me with stealing bikes and then, when we can't pay off our debts, he gets us to sell drugs."

What? Me sell drugs? Who to? I feel sick. Why didn't I walk away as soon as Dwayne talked about finding "product." And "runts." They were really just little kids—Katie's age. The image of Stevie in the back of the cop cruiser flashes through my mind. Then the gun to Danny's head. And suddenly I'm on my hands and knees at the side of the river, spewing my guts out. The pulled pork can't leave fast enough. I heave and puke, and when I hear in my mind the sick, wet, smacking sound of Dwayne beating up Danny, I heave again.

When I'm done, I realize Danny's gone, but I can hear him stumbling through the trees. I find my bike and take off after him. He's not too far ahead, limping badly.

"There's one thing I can't figure out," he says, as he hobbles along. I can tell he's trying to put distance between himself and the cops.

"What's that?"

"Why were *you* here? You normally pop up at drug deals?"

"I was at the Den," I say finally. "Outside. When they put you into the van, I followed."

Danny doesn't say anything for a while. His breath is loud and harsh in the darkness. Then, "I guess you don't want to let me ride that thing."

"No way. But there's a path ahead. Once we get there, I'll give you a lift on the handlebars."

We push through the trees and onto pavement. Danny climbs on and we wobble off. It was way more fun having Mandy up here. Danny reeks of sweat and old clothes. I pedal and pant. It's hard going. We turn off the bike path and into a back alley lined with garages and garbage cans. I slow to a stop. My knees are shaking.

"Danny, you gotta get off."

He slides from the bike and crumples onto the grass. "I don't think I can walk anymore," he says.

It must be close to midnight. We both need to get home, but I can't figure out a way to do it. In the darkness, my stomach growls loud enough to wake up the neighborhood. Katie says she's convinced I have bears in my belly. The bears used to be especially loud when our mother was making her chili. "The grizzlies need feeding," Katie would call out to the kitchen.

A bowl of Mom's chili would be great right now. Funny, I can practically smell it drifting along on the night air. I look around in case a pot of chili just happens to be sitting on a back porch.

That's when I see the Peugeot road bike inside a yard, leaning against a shed—unlocked.

I almost smile. My mother had an old white Peugeot that she loved. She was fifteen when she bought it new with babysitting money, and she had it until a few years ago when it was…stolen. I remember how upset she was.

But I'm not going to steal this bike. Just borrow it. So Danny and I can get home.

Chapter Nineteen

"Wait here," I say. "I'll get us a ride."

I unlatch the gate, make my way up the path and pull the bike away from the shed. That's when the motion-detector light switches on. Behind the shed, the sound of barking bursts into the night. The Peugeot isn't the only thing that's not chained down.

I drop the bike and run, but a dog grabs on to the leg of my jeans and won't let go. I try to shake it off, but it growls and snaps and bites even higher. And then this guy bursts out the back door of the house. He's big and meaty, and one huge hand clamps on to my bad shoulder while the other grabs the dog by the collar and shakes the animal.

"Grimm, that's enough. Heel. Grimm. Grimm!" The guy's voice matches his hand, which seems to be in contact with all the pain points in my shoulder. I want to sink into the ground, but the dog might chew my face off.

"Grimm! Enough! Kennel!" The dog lets go but keeps growling. The guy points behind the shed and the dog slinks away, still grumbling. Lights are coming on up and down the alley, and people are stepping outside to see what's going on.

"So, you little weasel, what are you doing with my bike?" The guy gives my shoulder a shake, and I nearly pass out. I gasp, but before I can say anything, a voice from the neighbor's yard cuts in.

"Nick? Nick! What are you doing here?" I look over. Mandy is running toward the fence. I groan. I want the ground to swallow me up, dog or no dog.

"You know this guy, Mandy? I'm pretty sure he was trying to steal my bike."

"Sure, we know him. This is Nick," says another voice. Now Ida's here too. "What's going on, Gordon?"

"I saw him grab my bike, but before I could do anything, Grimm caught him," the guy—Gordon—says.

"It's got to be a mistake," says Mandy. She slips through the gate and comes toward us.

Gordon swings me around to face her. "So tell her," he says. "Tell her what you were doing with my bike. Tell her why I shouldn't call the cops."

Mandy is looking at me, trying to read my face. Her hair is out of its ponytail, and it dances loose and soft across her shoulders. The floodlights make the dusting of freckles across her nose stand out. I want to touch them, connect them. I want to—

"Nick! Tell me. Tell Gordon. You didn't—"

Usually, I'm not the talkative type. I like to keep my mouth shut. Somehow, tonight, nothing's the same. I cut Mandy off. "I did. I did try to take this bike." She looks stunned.

"But…and…" My mouth suddenly has a mind of its own. It's not done. It's as if the puking just won't stop. "And I took yours too."

Horror, then fury, skitters across Mandy's face. She turns away from me.

"Auntie Ida, call the cops."

Chapter Twenty

It's bad enough that Mandy hates my guts now. But when the cops pull up in the alley to take me away, Danny's gone. With my fixie.

After an hour at the police station, a cop plunks a cheese sandwich down in front of me and I nearly dive into it, I'm so hungry. For some reason, I can't get my hands to stop shaking. I struggle to open the milk carton she puts next to the sandwich. I'm so busy trying to eat and drink that I don't look up when someone new walks in.

"What were you thinking?"

I freeze. In my mouth, the cheese sandwich turns to glue. Prickles of fear race along the back of my neck and under my arms. Shades is standing in front of me, sunglasses on the top of his head, scar twitching. How did he get away during the police takedown? Does that mean Trevor and Dwayne got away too?

"What possessed you to go riding right into a drug bust? Are you really that stupid?"

I swallow the gunk in my mouth. "What are you doing here?"

"I'm an undercover police officer. I'm Constable David Jones."

Before I can think things through, the door bursts open and Katie rushes in.

She flings herself at me. "Nick! Where have you been? Why didn't you come back? What are you doing here? I was so worried." And then my little sister does something weird. The kid who can take a soccer ball in the face or watch her brother come back from the dead without crying—ever—bursts into tears.

"Here, let's move to a bigger room," Shades says. Only now do I notice that both Mr. and Mrs. Radler are here. So is Kris, my social worker. We shuffle into another room, Katie welded to my side. For the next two hours, we go through everything that's happened.

It's like pulling scabs from festering sores.

That TV in your living room? *Rip*. Actually, it broke, and the one that's there belongs to someone else.

Those friends of yours at school? *Rip*. I was training them to be little criminals.

All that time when I was supposed to be at school? *Rip*. I was really stealing bikes—lots of bikes, not just the one from tonight.

Rip, yank, rip.

The only thing I don't talk about is Mandy, because really, there's nothing to talk about. At the end of it all, I feel as if I've been bled dry.

The room is silent while Shades—Constable Jones—steps outside with Kris. The Radlers look stunned. I can't blame them. Who'd want someone like me under their roof? Katie is curled up at my side, asleep.

Constable Jones comes back in. "Trevor Glatzen and Dwayne Borowski have just been charged with a number of offenses, including assault, kidnapping, possession, trafficking and a whole raft of weapons charges. They're being transferred to the remand center, where they'll be held until their trial."

"Will Nick have to testify?" Mrs. Radler asks.

"I'm not sure. It depends on how the case builds up," he says. Then he looks at Katie and me. "I think it's time you take them home," he says to the Radlers.

I swallow. "You mean, I can leave?"

"I'll be by tomorrow when you get home from school," he says, emphasizing the last six words. "Do I make myself clear?"

I nod.

The Radlers are both on their feet before I get up. Mr. Radler comes close and puts a hand on my shoulder. Is he trying to keep me from going with them?

"Look at me, Nick," he says. I look up. This is it, I figure. Katie and I are going to be split up. "The next time you're in trouble over something like a stupid TV, you come to us. Got it?"

I nod. So does he. Then he scoops up Katie from beside me. But I can't pry her fingers from my T-shirt. Even in her sleep, it seems like she can't bear to let me go.

Chapter Twenty-One

Without my bike, I have to get up even earlier to make it to school on time. Only my math teacher says anything to me about being away for almost a week. "Test on Monday, Nick. See me at lunch."

My body feels like that dog from last night chewed all of me up and spat me out. I limp from class to class, and when the last bell rings, I think seriously about sneaking onto a city bus to get home. But I'm in enough trouble as it is. Instead, I head past the bike racks, just in case my fixie's there. It's not.

All day, I've been thinking about life without my bike. No more flying through the city, no more burning off energy, no more freedom. And it burns me to think that Danny's riding the bike I put together with my dad, and I won't ever be able to put another one together with him. A wave of grief pounds into my chest, and I have to stop moving just so I can catch my breath. It's not fair, I want to shout. It's just not fair. I can feel my eyes prickle, but I will...not...cry.

"Hey, Dickhead." Danny pulls up beside me. On my fixie. I stop and glare at him. He looks way better than he did last night. For one thing, he's cleaned up. But there's a cast on his arm and stitches above his lip.

"Hey, Fat Lip," I say.

He starts to grin, then stops. I can tell it's pulling on his stitches. His eyes are still dancing. "Yeah, but by next week my face will be back to normal, and you'll still be a dickhead."

"You know, it was that lip of yours that got you beat up last night," I say. "I was there, at the door."

The smile in his eyes switches off. "Yeah, well." Both of us are remembering. Finally, Danny gets off my bike.

"So, you never, ever thought about putting a backup hand brake on this thing?"

I shake my head. "Nah. I like going full tilt."

"I'd build mine with an aluminum frame and a shorter fork," he says.

"Depends on what you want it for. I could show you…" And then I stop. I was going to say that I could show him a fork at the Den that would work perfectly for him. But I remember.

"What's the matter? You don't want to show me?" Danny's voice has an edge to it.

"No, it's not that. It's just that the Den's closed now. That's all over."

Danny nods, hands me my bike and turns away.

But I'm thinking about all the bike parts at the Den. Some of them might go back to the original owners, but there're lots there that won't find a home. What a waste to throw it all out. What about…

"Hey, Fat Lip. Wait a second," I say, and Danny turns around. "You need to be somewhere this afternoon?"

He shakes his head. An idea is forming in mine.

"There's someone you need to meet," I say.

Chapter Twenty-Two

Turns out Constable Jones and Danny already know each other. Of course, they met when Shades was undercover and I brought in the wrong Yeti. But the constable tracked Danny down early this morning and sat with him in the hospital waiting room while the doctors stitched him together again.

"Hey, Jonesy," Danny says as we climb the porch steps at the Radler house. Constable Jones is parked in one of the plastic chairs, and Kris is in the other. A box of donuts sits open between them.

Jonesy hands us the box, and we grab two donuts each. My mouth is watering, but I don't take a bite. "Look, before we get into everything, can you guys answer a question?"

"Fire away," Kris says.

"What's going to happen to the Den? I mean, the stuff that's in the Den?"

"Well, we'll see whether any of the property can be returned to its rightful owners. But some of it might be hard to identify," says Jonesy, looking right at me. "In fact, you can work off the community-service hours you're going to get by putting some of those bikes back together again."

I flush and nod, then keep going. "Look. If there's any stuff left over once we're done, can I—no, can *we* have it? Danny doesn't have a bike, and I thought I would show him how to build one. With the leftover parts. And can we still use the Den?"

Jonesy and Kris don't say anything for a while, so I bite into my chocolate-covered donut, just so the icing doesn't melt.

"Looks like we're all chewing on something," says Danny. He's almost finished his second apple fritter.

"I think we can make that work," Kris says finally. "I'm not so sure about the building—"

Jonesy cuts in. "We tracked down the owner early this morning. He had no idea Glatzen had set up a chop shop in there. If you set up a community group"—he looks at Kris—"I'll bet he'd rent it out for next to nothing.

Maybe that would bring in other businesses."

Kris is nodding. "I know some people at a local bike society who would probably volunteer for this…"

"What are you guys talking about?" Katie pulls up on her bike and sets her backpack down. She has a new button on it—a grizzly with a feather pen, called Shakesbear. I wonder if it's from Alex, and if she still talks to him.

"A place where Nick and Danny can build a bike," says Kris.

"Just Nick and Danny? I know of at least two other people who want to learn," Katie says as steps up to the donut box.

I frown. "There's Alex," I say, "but Stevie's moved."

"I want to learn too, you know." She brushes past us to her bike, which is lying by the bottom step. She parks herself beside it and starts picking the blue sprinkles off her donut. This used to drive Mom nuts, I remember.

"So, a kind of a bike school," says Jonesy.

Danny jumps in. "Yeah. A place where we could build, or fix, our own bikes."

"I bet we could get people to give us their old bikes for this. And companies could donate stock that hasn't sold by the end of the season." Kris is sounding excited.

"But you guys need to clean the place up," Jonesy says.

The three of us nod. "Wait till I tell Alex," Katie says. She's finished her donut. Now she's holding her napkin over the spokes of her front tire and spinning the wheel wildly. It makes a great *flut-flut-flut* noise. "And I'll finally get to see the Den," she says.

"I'm not too keen..." Jonesy pauses. Katie lifts the napkin, now covered in bike dirt, from the wheel and looks up. "On the Den as a name," he finishes. "It needs something fresh."

Katie lets her finger run across the slender rods that hold her wheel together. "The Spoke," she says.

"I like it," says Jonesy. Kris nods.

"The girl has spoke-en," Danny says. Katie throws the dirty napkin at him.

Chapter Twenty-Three

Word spreads, and by Saturday morning there's at least a dozen of us gathered when Kris unlocks the new front door of the Spoke. A guy from a glass company has just finished putting in new windows. It makes a huge difference. I can see the whole space, and in my mind's eye, I can see what it will look like when we're done.

We haul out garbage and sort through bike parts. Danny finds three road-bike frames stuffed behind one of the counters. Katie uncovers a box of pedals that has never been opened. And this other kid—Julie—finds a brand-new set of bike tires. When she shows them to us, a streak of joy flashes through me.

That's when Alex catches my eye. He's been avoiding me, working at the other end. But when Julie brings the tires to the front, Alex follows her. "Those are from the bike I stole from that high school. That big dude got you to take them off. I thought he was going to sell them."

"Probably hadn't found a buyer yet," says Danny.

"Can I use them?" Alex asks.

I shake my head. "No. They're going back on the original bike. It's still here."

"And then can I have it? I was the one who took it in the first place," Alex says.

I shake my head again. "No. The bike is going back to its owner."

Alex looks at me suspiciously. "Yeah, right. What are you going to do? Look for the first klutzy girl and say, 'Here, I took this from you, but now you can have it back'?"

The wail of a police siren cuts off my answer. A cruiser pulls up outside, and the flashing lights strobe through the front windows. Three of the kids drop what they're doing and melt out the back way.

A cop steps out of the vehicle, carrying four huge pizza boxes. He looks familiar, but it's not until he walks in that I recognize him. It's Jonesy, minus the long, greasy hair and dressed in full cop uniform.

"I was worried you guys were running out of steam. This might keep you going," he says.

But I have no time for pizza. I dig out Mandy's bike frame, put the tires back on and pump them up. The brake pads on the back wheel are worn, so I look for a new set and install them. I replace all the cables and clean and lube the chain. I wipe the whole bike down and push it out the front door.

"Where are you going, Nick?" Katie calls out.

"I won't be too long," I say. "I just need to give something back."

Acknowledgments

The Spoke really exists and was one of the inspirations for *Bike Thief.* Social worker Kris Andreychuk helped establish this Edmonton workspace, where kids can learn how to build and maintain their own bikes. I am grateful for his time and enthusiasm and for his putting me in touch with the real Constable David Jones. As a member of Edmonton Police Service's Child at Risk Response Team, Constable Jones generously answered all my questions about policing and bike theft.

I would also like to thank avid cyclists Ben Appelt and Meika Ellis, who were wonderful sources of information about fixies, velodromes and bicycles in general. Any errors of fact are mine.

Finally, to Gordon, Emma and Sarah, for their support, readings and loud, sprawling reenactments of crucial scenes, my love and thanks always.

Rita Feutl has always loved bikes. At the age of seven, she wrecked an Easter dress by greasing her bicycle before church. When she was fifteen, Rita bought a white Peugeot, which she owned for decades. It died in a garage fire. Now she speeds along backcountry byways on a Giant road bike. When she's not cycling all over Canada and Europe, Rita lives with her family in Edmonton, Alberta, where four of their bikes have been stolen (one of them twice!). *Bike Thief* is Rita's third book. For more information, visit www.ritafeutl.com.

orca soundings

For more information on all the books
in the Orca Soundings series, please visit
www.orcabook.com.